For Kitty

First published 1987 by
Walker Books Ltd
184-192 Drummond Street
London NW1 3HP

©1987 Sarah Garland

First printed 1987
Printed and bound by L.E.G.O., Vicenza, Italy

British Library Cataloguing in Publication Data
Garland, Sarah
Sam's cat.
I. Title
823'.914[J]   PZ7

ISBN 0-7445-0705-7

SAM'S CAT

Sarah Garland

WALKER BOOKS
LONDON

Our cat is getting very fat.

She must be going to have kittens.

My family is not very excited.

They are all so busy.

Aren't they interested in kittens?

I'll just zoom down the garden
to my shed.

I'll make a special bed for the
kittens to be born in.

Now I must find the cat.

I hope she'll be pleased with her new bed.

But where can she be?
She's vanished!

Is she having her kittens all alone
in the cold dark night?

What's this in my bottom drawer?

The babies are born!

My family is quite excited now.

I think I'll turn this cat bed
into a robot.